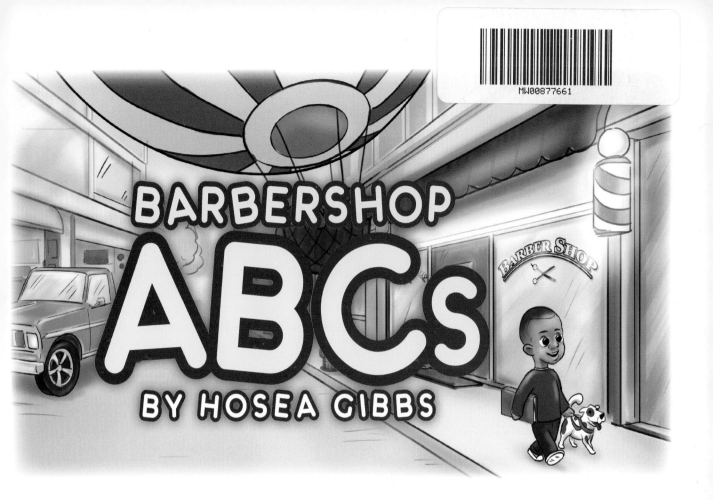

BARBERSHOP ABCs
BY HOSEA GIBBS

Illustrations by Nicolas Spinelli

Details
PUBLISHING

Atlanta, GA

Barbershop ABCs: My 1st Class
Copyright © 2017 Hosea Gibbs

Address inquiries to the publisher:

Details Publishing
P.O. Box 5704
Atlanta, GA 31107 USA

Learn more about the author at
www.BarbershopABCs.com

ISBN: 978-0-9988023-0-5 (hardback)
ISBN: 978-0-9988023-2-9 (paperback)
ISBN: 978-0-9988023-1-2 (ebook)

Library of Congress Control Number: 2017939391

Illustrations by Nicolas Spinelli
Edited by Annette Johnson, Allwrite Communications Inc.
Cover by Joey Shephard, QJS Design Studio

Printed in the PRC.

Dedication

I would like to dedicate this book to my wonderful kids: Kennedy and Robert Gibbs. My prayer is that you both put God first in every decision you make.

I want to thank my wife, Whitney L. Gibbs, for her support in this process.

In general, I want to thank every teacher, barber/stylist, parent, and school everywhere for sharing the lessons in this book with the children in your life.

Hi, my name is **Bobby**, and I learned my ABCs at the barbershop. Now you can learn them too like I did.

Aa

is for *ask*

My dad, Bob, says you should always **ask** how many people are in line in front of you. If you know how many people are in front of you, you will know how long you will have to wait before you can get your hair cut.

Bb is for *barber*

I see my **barber** every Thursday. Sometimes I even make an appointment.

Cc is for *chair*

I am not allowed to play in the barber's **chair**. It could be dangerous.

Dd

is for *dog*

My **dog**, Lucky, is not allowed in the barbershop. The sign in the window says that I have to "leave pets outside" if I bring them with me.

Ee

is for *edge*

When I get a razor **edge**, my haircut lasts longer. I like the way my hair looks in the mirror when it's done.

Ff is for *fun*

I have **fun** at the barbershop. Sometimes I watch people play games while I wait to get my hair cut.

Gg is for *good*

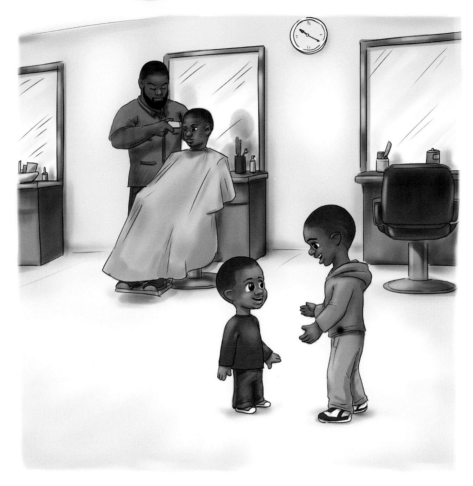

I meet new, **good** friends, like Todd, at the barbershop.

Hh is for *head*

My barber asks me to take my hat off so he can see my **head**.

Ii is for *image*

At my school, we must have a neat **image**, so my hair always has to be cut.

Jj is for *job*

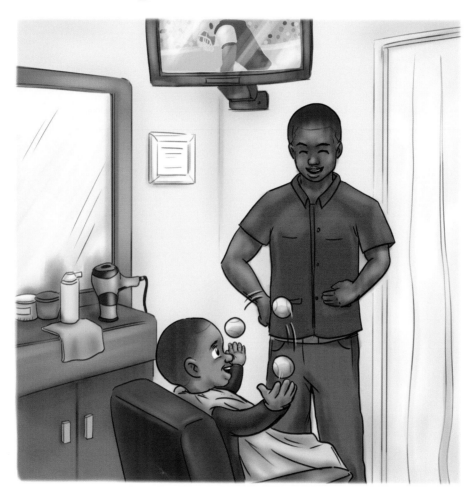

My barber does his **job** well. He has lots of skills. He even taught me how to juggle.

Kk is for *kind*

My barber is very **kind**, and he knows a lot.
He talks to me about all kinds of things.

Ll is for *line*

My barber takes his time to **line** my hair, and
I have to sit very still.

Mm is for *mom*

Sometimes my **mom** holds my hand in the barbershop.

Nn is for *noise*

Sometimes the clippers make a scary **noise**
I don't like, but I try to sit there like a big boy.

Oo is for *open*

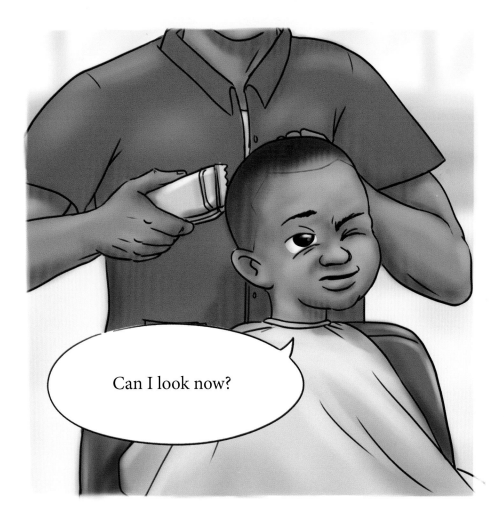

I try to keep my eyes **open** when I get a haircut.

Pp

is for *pay*

I **pay** my barber a little extra for his service, which is called a "tip," when he does a really good job.

Qq is for *quiet*

Sometimes the barbershop is **quiet**, and sometimes it's not.

Rr is for *read*

My sister, Kennedy, likes to **read** at the barbershop when she comes with me.

Ss is for *sweep*

I love to **sweep** up the hair at the barbershop
to keep it clean.

Tt is for *toy*

My barber always has a **toy** for me when I get my haircut.

Uu is for *unique*

My barbershop has a **unique** place where we wash our hands. I have to be very careful.

Vv is for *video*

I often watch a **video** while I wait at the barbershop.

Ww is for *wash*

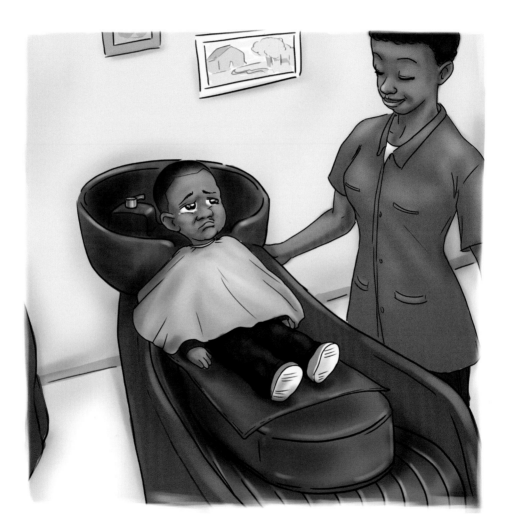

I **wash** my hair after getting a haircut
because my mom likes it nice and clean.

Xx is for *xylophone*

Sometimes I bring my **xylophone** and play it at the barbershop.

Yy is for *young*

I learn so much from both the **young** and the old people in the barbershop.

Zz is for *zap*

I have to sit still in the barber's chair or
I might get **zapped**!

Here is some more **barbershop vocabulary**, including the ABCs already mentioned, that Bobby wants to share with you:

Ask	Edge	Kind
Barber	Extra	Line
Brush	Friend	Mom
Chair	Fun	Mirror
Clippers	Good	Noise
Comb	Hair	Open
Cut	Hat	Pay
Dad	Head	Pet
Dog	Image	Quiet
Dye	Job	Razor

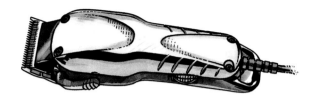

Read

Rinse

Scissors

Shears

Still

Sweep

Tip

Toy

Unique

Video

Wait

Wash

Xylophone

Young

Zap